Daddy's SURPRISE Christmas

Written by Susan Karnovsky

Illustrated by Design 5

It was almost Christmas — and Bryan was sad.
His dad was too busy again.

"He never has time for me," Bryan whispered.

"He's a famous scientist, Bryan," his mother said.

When his dad got off the phone he said "I've got to leave right away."

"I understand," his mother sighed. "I'll be waiting for you here."

I won't! Bryan decided. *I'm going with you!*

An hour later, a special limousine was there to pick up Bryan's father. Nobody noticed Bryan. Everyone was too busy.

He climbed in to a special crate. It was padded and air conditioned. It was designed to hold very sensitive measuring equipment. But there was lots of room for Bryan.

The limousine drove to the airport.

No one knew Bryan
was aboard.

Inside the crate, Bryan fell asleep.

When he woke up, Bryan couldn't believe
what he saw.

It was his daddy with *Santa Claus*!
"What are you doing here?" his father demanded.
"I..I..I..." Bryan couldn't get any words out.

"You shouldn't be here!" his father said.
"There's not a second to lose," Santa said.
"Get out of the crate," Bryan's father said.
"Here, let me help you," Santa said.

Bryan watched his father walk off with
Santa. Everyone seemed so busy.

"Dad— "

"Not now, Bryan. I'm too busy. Go play
with the elves in the workshop!"

Santa's fancy new super sleigh wasn't
working. There was no time to lose!

"What's wrong with the sleigh?" Bryan asked an elf who was passing by.

"We don't know," the elf said. "We built it bigger and better than ever. But the test flights were too low and too slow. That's why we called your father.

Bryan went back to the workshop. Everyone
there was busy too. He picked up a paintbrush and
went to work. But he wished he could be with his dad.

Later that afternoon he went back to the
lab where his dad was working.

But Bryan could see his dad was still too
busy to talk to him.

"My elves could use some help wrapping
presents," Santa kindly suggested.

Bryan went back to the workshop. He helped the elves wrap presents.

But he would rather have been with his dad.

His dad was busier than ever. He still didn't
know what was wrong with the sleigh. Time was
running out.

Now he was testing the secret fuel formula
that the reindeer ate to help them fly.

Bryan followed the elf into the kitchen. He watched while busy elves mixed and cooked reindeer food.

Meanwhile, back in the lab, Santa and Bryan's father were busy searching for the problem.

Bryan knew he couldn't bother his father.
He walked outside into the cold air. Across from
the workshop he saw the reindeer stables. Elves
were there, busy like everywhere else.

Bryan stepped inside. There were all the famous reindeer.

"Hello," Bryan said.

Prancer shook his head *hello*. Dancer stomped a hoof. Donner winked. Rudolph blinked his red nose.

"You guys are the first ones to have any time to talk to me. Everyone's so busy here," Brian told them.

"I know," Prancer agreed "It wasn't always like this."

Bryan ran back to the lab. Santa and his father looked tired and worried.

"Dad, I think I found the problem. It's not the sleigh, it's the reindeer. They told me they're very sad because Santa's too busy to spend any time with them." Bryan's dad and Santa looked at each other and smiled.

The reindeer were excited to see Santa.
Santa was happy to see them too. He didn't realize how
much he had missed them. He hugged each one and
talked to them for a long time.

Bryan and his father looked happily at Santa
and his reindeers.

"Thanks, Bryan," his father said. "You solved
the problem. You're daddy's best helper."

It was almost Christmas — and Bryan felt
very, very, happy.